The Riddle of the Robin

By Valerie Tripp
Illustrated by Thu Thai

American Girl®

Published by American Girl Publishing

16 17 18 19 20 21 22 LEO 10 9 8 7 6 5 4 3 2

Editorial Development: Jodi Goldberg and Jennifer Hirsch
Art Direction and Design: Riley Wilkinson and Jessica Annoye
Production: Jeannette Bailey, Mary Makarushka, Cynthia Stiles, and Kristi Tabrizi
Vignettes on pages 90–93 by Flavia Conley

For Brody Granger Dawson,
with love

The WellieWishers are a group of fun-loving girls who each have the same big, bright wish: to be a good friend. They love to play in a large and leafy backyard garden cared for by Willa's Aunt Miranda.

When the WellieWishers step into their colorful garden boots, also known as wellingtons or *wellies*, they are ready for anything—stomping in mud puddles, putting on a show, and helping friendships grow. Like you, they're learning that being kind, creative, and caring isn't always easy, but it's the best way to make friendships bloom.

GARDEN MAP
Carrot's Hutch
Playhouse
Garden Gate
Aunt Miranda's House
Garden Theater Stage

Pond
N
W
E
S
Garden Shed
Tea Table
Veggie Garden

A Fine Feathered Friend

Willa was excited. She danced a happy little jig of impatience while she waited for her friends, the WellieWishers. She had something wonderful to show them!

Kendall, Ashlyn, Camille, and Emerson came into the garden. "Hi, Willa!" they said.

"Hi!" said Willa. "Hurry and put on your wellies. I've got a surprise for you."

"That's wonderful," said Emerson. "I *love* surprises!"

"What is it?" asked Camille. She was hop, hop, hopping on one foot as she pulled her wellington boot onto the other foot. Carrot, the pet bunny, hippety-hopped along next to Camille.

Willa led the way to the maple tree. "Look," she said.

There, nestled cozily between the roots, was a brave little bright yellow flower. The WellieWishers crouched around it.

"Oh, it's so cute!" said Ashlyn.

"It's a crocus," said Willa, "and it means that spring is here."

"Spring!" crowed Emerson, bouncing up to her feet. "Spring is my favorite season. I love everything spring-y. I'm spring-y myself!" She began to bounce and boing up and down like a spring. *Boingeddy, boingeddy, boing, boing, boing!*

"I like spring, too," said Kendall. "Especially March." She laughed and pretended to play a flute as she marched in place. "Come on, let's march! Hup, two, three, four. Hup, two, three, four."

Everyone marched. Carrot hopped behind them to join the fun.

Suddenly, a cheery whistle filled the air, as if a piccolo player had joined their pretend parade: *Too-wheet!*

"Shhh," shushed Willa, holding her hand to her ear and tilting her head to listen.

"What's that?" whispered Emerson.

Willa smiled. "I think it's another sign of spring," she whispered back.

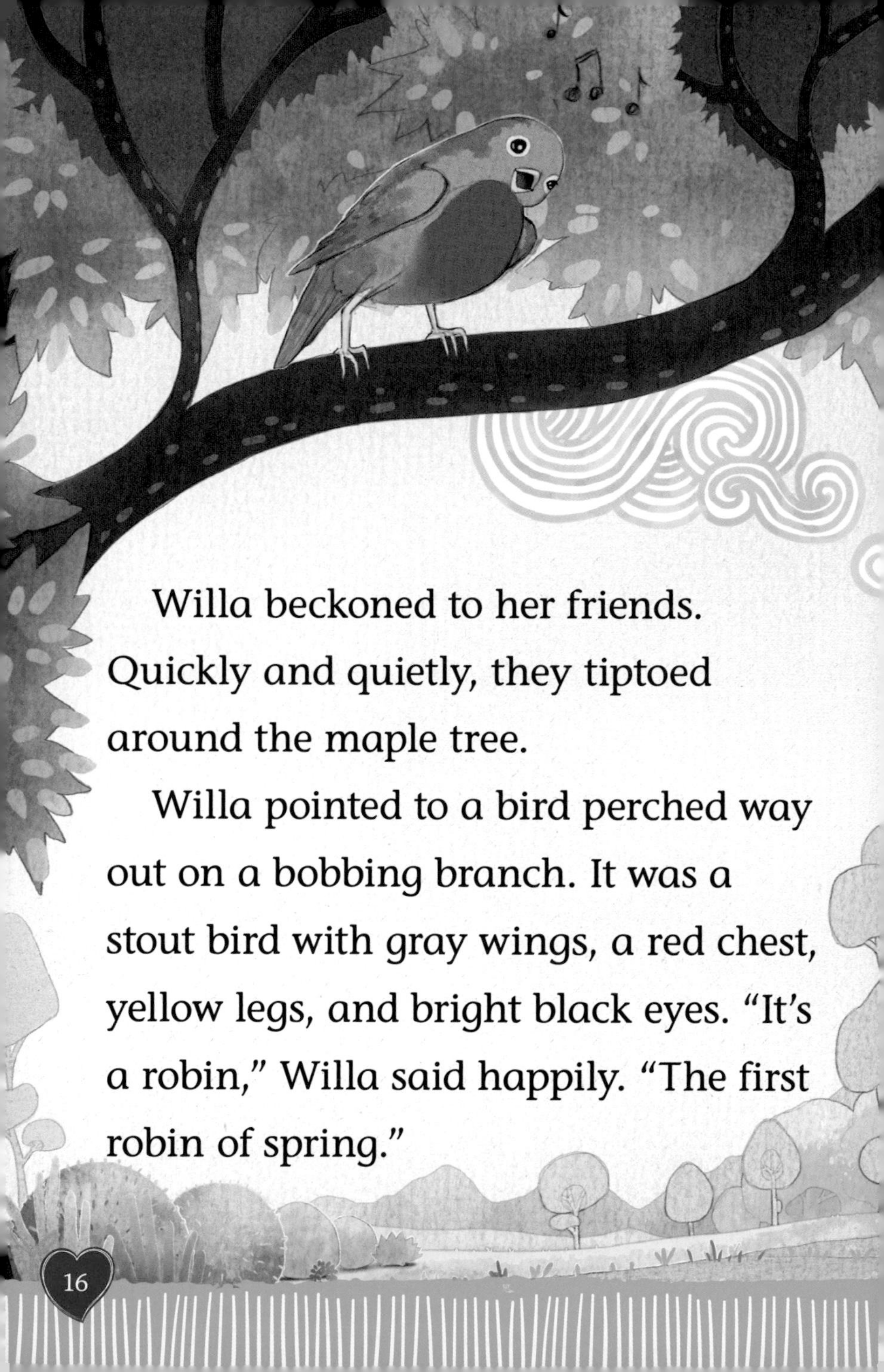

Willa beckoned to her friends. Quickly and quietly, they tiptoed around the maple tree.

Willa pointed to a bird perched way out on a bobbing branch. It was a stout bird with gray wings, a red chest, yellow legs, and bright black eyes. "It's a robin," Willa said happily. "The first robin of spring."

"Oooooh," cooed the girls.

The friendly robin cocked its head and looked at the girls. *"Too-wheet,"* the robin chirped proudly, as if to say, "Oh yes, you are quite right to admire me. I am very good-looking indeed."

"Look how shiny the robin's red chest feathers are," said Camille.

"It looks like it's wearing a fancy red vest," said Ashlyn.

"Too-wheet, too-wheet?" tweeted the robin, as if it were asking a question.

"Yes, absolutely, *too-wheet,*" Willa answered politely. "Please stay. Welcome to the garden."

The girls didn't think Willa was silly to talk to a bird. Willa understood animals, and this robin seemed to understand Willa perfectly.

The robin puffed out its red chest, lifted its little bill, and sang.

Emerson rose up on her toes and flapped her hands excitedly. "I've made up a song," she announced. She stood under the tree and flung her arms out wide. Looking up at the robin, she sang to the tune of "Mary Had a Little Lamb":

Sing to us your song so sweet,
Song so sweet, song so sweet.
Sing to us your song so sweet:
Too-wheet, too-wheet, too-wheet.

Since you're back we know it's spring,
Know it's spring, know it's spring.
Since you're back we know it's spring.
Too-wheet, too-wheet, too-wheet.

As if delighted, the robin fluttered its feathers and trilled with gusto—

Emerson smiled and said, "It's fun to sing along with a fine feathered friend like our robin!"

Gifts for the Robin

The next day after school, the WellieWishers rushed to the garden as fast as they could. They were eager to see their friend the robin.

"I hope it's waiting for us," said Willa.

"It is," said Camille. "Look!"

The robin was perched on the same skinny branch as the day before. The girls slowed down when they came near, so they wouldn't frighten the robin.

"Hello, Robin," said Ashlyn. "How are you today?"

"*Brrr-eeet!*" chirped the robin.

"That's good," said Willa. "Look, everyone, I brought a bird book."

"And we brought a birdfeeder, birdseed, and a bird water dish," said Camille, Ashlyn, and Kendall.

"And I brought a bird hat!" said Emerson.

Willa smiled. “It was nice of you to bring things to make the robin feel at home here,” she said.

“Let’s give them to the robin,” said Kendall.

Ashlyn put birdseed in the birdfeeder. Camille put water in the dish for the robin to drink. Emerson put on the bird hat. Kendall hung the

birdfeeder in the maple tree.

"Your restaurant is open, Robin," said Willa, bowing and gesturing toward the birdfeeder.

At first, the robin seemed curious. It swooped down and hovered near the feeder. It flew above it, below it, and all around it in a circle. Then the robin flew right back and landed

on its same old branch without eating anything. *"Brrrt,"* it chirruped, sounding unimpressed.

"Why isn't the robin using any of our gifts?" asked Camille sadly.

"Probably it's just not used to them yet," said Ashlyn.

"Or maybe there's something wrong with them," said Kendall.

Willa was looking at her bird book. "It says here that robins don't eat birdseed, so they don't go to birdfeeders."

"Ohhhh," said the girls.

“That’s too bad,” said Ashlyn. “I wanted to give our robin some food, so it’ll know that we’re its friend.”

“What *do* robins eat?” asked Kendall. “Maybe we could find some food for our robin here in the garden.”

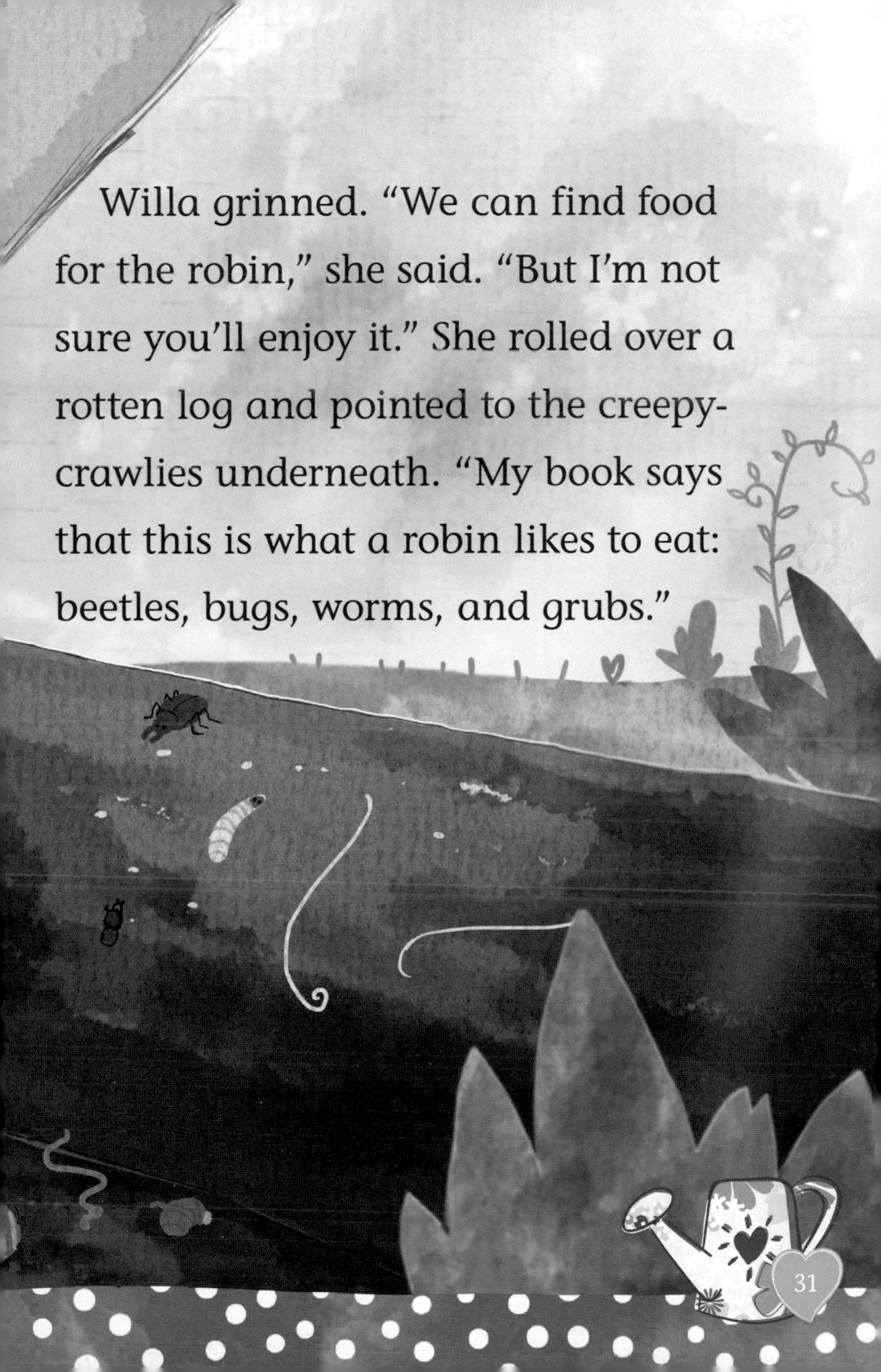

Willa grinned. "We can find food for the robin," she said. "But I'm not sure you'll enjoy it." She rolled over a rotten log and pointed to the creepy-crawlies underneath. "My book says that this is what a robin likes to eat: beetles, bugs, worms, and grubs."

"*Ew!*" said the WellieWishers.

Camille recited a little jingle that she made up:

> Beetles, bugs, worms, and grubs:
> That sounds sooooo delicious.
> Beetles, bugs, worms, and grubs.
> Our robin's favorite dishes!

Ashlyn wrinkled her nose. "I don't think I like those beetles," she said.

"Beetles are hardworking bugs," said Willa. "They chew dead wood and help to break it into little bits, so that it can become part of the dirt. And they're food for birds."

"Oh, yum," joked Emerson. "So, shall we make our robin a lovely lunch? A dish of worm spaghetti, with a side order of squooshed bugs and grubs, and some nice icky beetles for dessert?"

"Ohh-kay," said Ashlyn, making a brave face.

"You mean, '*Eww*-kay,'" giggled Camille.

And all the girls recited Camille's jingle:

> Beetles, bugs, worms, and grubs:
> That sounds sooooo delicious.
> Beetles, bugs, worms, and grubs.
> Our robin's favorite dishes!

But the creepy-crawlies didn't bother Willa at all. She made a little cup out of two leaves and gathered some worms, lifting them gently with her fingertips. Then she collected a few big beetles.

Willa put the worms and beetles in a little pile on the cupped leaves below the tree. “I hope you’re hungry, Robin,” she said.

All the girls stepped back. They stood still so that they wouldn't scare the robin. After a little while, the robin flitted down and picked up a worm. Then it flew back up to its branch with the worm dangling from its beak.

"Enjoy that wiggly-weggly wormy spaghetti," said Camille to the robin.

"With some yummy gummy muddy sauce!" laughed Ashlyn. "Sooooo delicious!"

Splish, Splash

While the robin ate, Kendall took the birdfeeder down from its branch. She tossed the birdseed onto the ground for another animal to eat, and she put the water dish at the bottom of the maple tree.

Suddenly, with a swish of wings, the robin swept down and sat, *sploop!* in the dish of water. With happy *splish-splashes,* the robin began to take a bath. Over and over again, the robin dipped its head into the water, fluttered its wings, and wiggled its tail feathers. The water spluttered up around it.

Ashlyn poked Kendall. “There, you see, Kendall?” she said with a smile. “The robin is using your gift—as a birdbath!”

“A birdbath! I *love* it!” said Emerson. She pretended to be the robin taking a very splishy, splashy bath. She dipped her head, fluttered her arms as if they were wings, and wiggled all over.

In fact, Emerson shook and fluttered her arms and legs so much that . . .

. . . one of her wellies flew off. Up it went into the air, twisting and turning, until it landed with a thud on the roof of the playhouse.

"Oops," said Emerson, staring at her boot up on the roof.

"Uh-oh," said Camille. "Your boot is too high up on the roof for us to get it down. We'll have to ask Aunt Miranda to get it down with a ladder."

"Don't worry, Emerson," said Ashlyn. "Meanwhile, you can borrow one of my extra wellies that I keep in the playhouse."

"Thanks," said Emerson. She grinned. "That's what I get for wearing boots in the bathtub. I was a birdbrain in the birdbath!"

Oh, No! Where'd It Go?

Every day, the robin perched on its favorite branch in the maple tree and greeted the WellieWishers when they came to the garden. Ashlyn got used to picking up worms and beetles, and she helped Kendall and Willa collect food for the robin. Camille kept its birdbath full of water. And Emerson led them all in singing to the tune of "Mary Had a Little Lamb":

Sing to us your song so sweet,
Song so sweet, song so sweet.
Sing to us your song so sweet:
Too-wheet, too-wheet, too-wheet.

Since you're back we know it's spring,
Know it's spring, know it's spring.
Since you're back we know it's spring.
Too-wheet, too-wheet, too-wheet.

And the robin would always sing back with great gusto, *"Too-wheet, too-wheet, too-wheet!"*

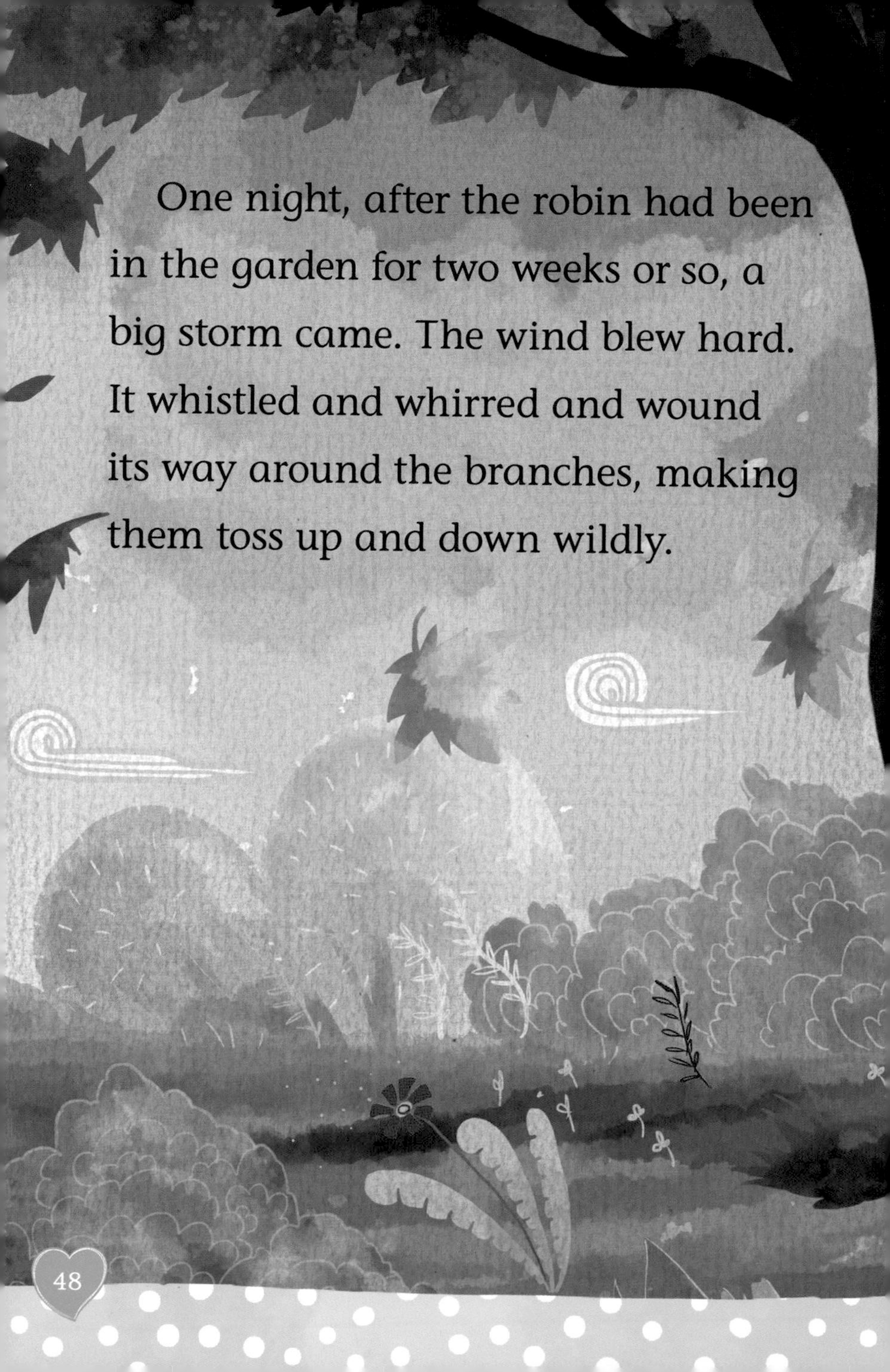

One night, after the robin had been in the garden for two weeks or so, a big storm came. The wind blew hard. It whistled and whirred and wound its way around the branches, making them toss up and down wildly.

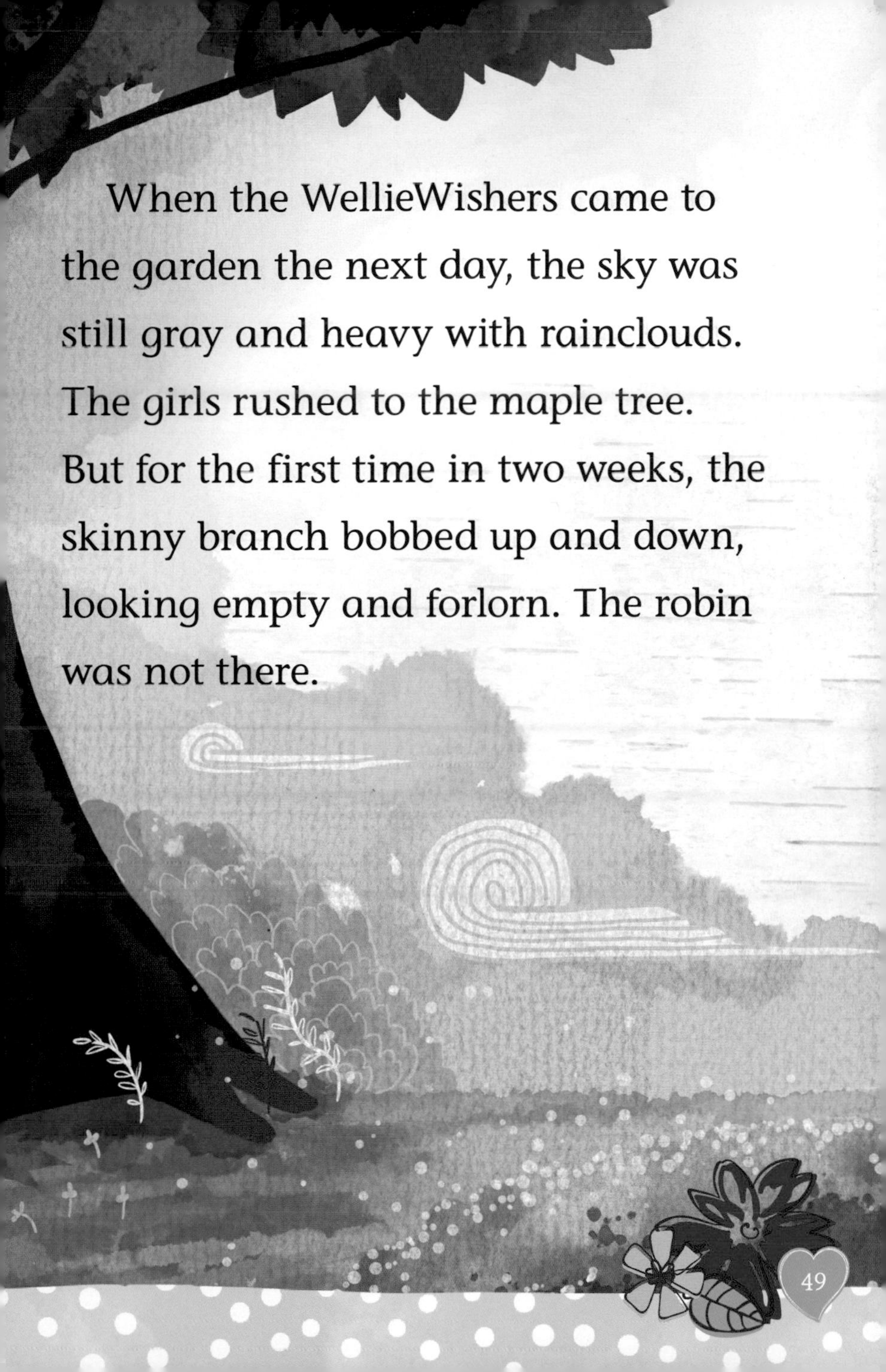

When the WellieWishers came to the garden the next day, the sky was still gray and heavy with rainclouds. The girls rushed to the maple tree. But for the first time in two weeks, the skinny branch bobbed up and down, looking empty and forlorn. The robin was not there.

Desperately, the girls searched all around the maple tree and the playhouse.

But there was no answer. The robin was gone.

Following Willa

Oh, dear," said Camille. "Do you think our robin is gone forever?"

"Maybe it flew to another part of the garden," said Willa, "where it felt safer during the storm."

"It might be hurt," said Ashlyn, "or lost."

"Let's go look for it," said Emerson. Willa rushed into the playhouse. She hung her binoculars around her neck and tucked her bird book, a map of the garden, and her compass into her backpack. She put granola bars, her canteen full of water, and cups in her backpack, too. Then she rushed back outside again.

"Is everybody ready?" Willa asked.

"Yes!" said the WellieWishers. "Let's go!" And off they went.

"Do you think we can find our robin?" asked Ashlyn as Willa led the girls deeper into Aunt Miranda's garden.

"If we keep our eyes open," said Willa. "And look carefully at all the trees and bushes and plants."

"What's this plant?" asked Camille, stooping down.

"Watch out!" warned Willa. "That's poison ivy, and it's trouble."

Camille jumped away so quickly that she fell backwards over a log and landed—*thump!*—on her bottom.

"Are you hurt?" asked Kendall kindly as she helped Camille stand up.

"No," said Camille, brushing off her skirt. She joked, "But that poison ivy caused me trouble, and I didn't even touch it!"

The girls walked quietly, looking high and low for the robin.

"Oh!" exclaimed Kendall. She tugged on Willa's sleeve and pointed up. "Look, a nest! Do you think it belongs to *our* robin?"

Willa looked at the nest through her binoculars. Then she gave her binoculars to the other girls so that they could take turns using them, too, while she looked in her bird book.

"That's not a robin's nest," she said. "That's a wood duck's nest." Willa showed the girls the picture in her bird book of a wood duck on its nest.

“A duck built a nest in a tree?” said Kendall.

“That’s kind of quackers,” joked Ashlyn.

“Quackers, crackers,” said Emerson. “I’m getting hungry. Can we have our snacks now?”

"Maybe you could eat like a bird," said Camille with a smile. "You know—

Beetles, bugs, worms, and grubs:
That sounds sooooo delicious!

"No, thank you," said Emerson firmly.

Willa looked around. The muddy ground was soggy with puddles. "It's too wet to sit here," she said. "Let's go back and sit on the benches near the playhouse to eat our snacks."

"But I'm hungry *now*," said Emerson.

"And I'm tired," said Kendall.

"And we haven't found our robin yet," added Ashlyn.

Willa tried to cheer her friends up. "Maybe the robin is back in the maple tree waiting for us right now," she said. "Let's go see!"

"Which is the way back?" asked Camille.

Willa looked around. "I'm not sure," she said. "We went off the path when we saw the duck's nest."

Emerson slumped onto a tree stump. "My feet are tired," she grumped. "I bet we walked a *hundred miles* looking for our robin! And now we'll have to walk *two* hundred miles to get home."

Kendall spoke quietly to Willa. "You know the way home, right, Willa?"

"Oh, no," said Ashlyn. "I can't believe it. We're lost!"

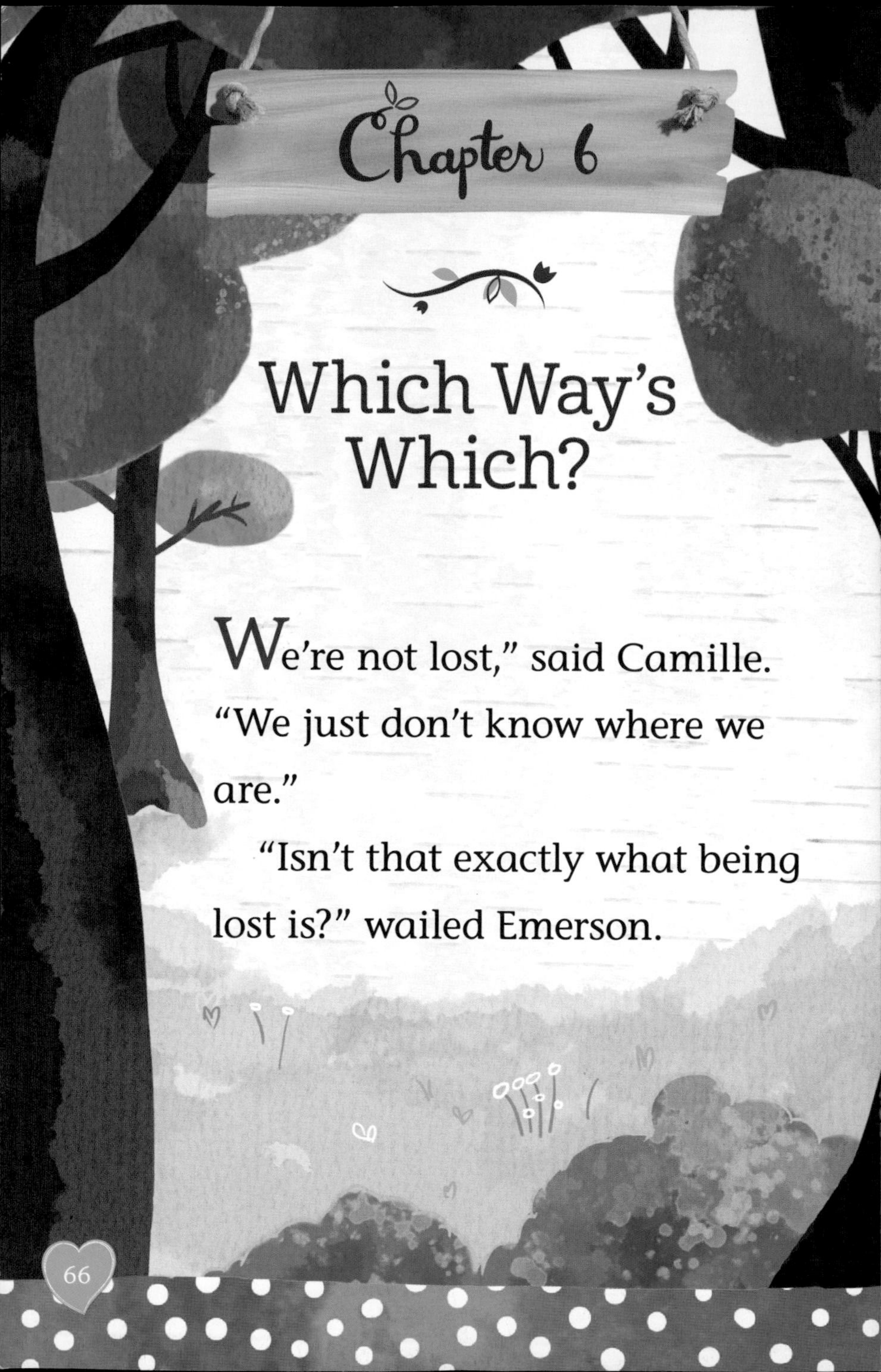

Chapter 6

Which Way's Which?

We're not lost," said Camille. "We just don't know where we are."

"Isn't that exactly what being lost is?" wailed Emerson.

"We're not lost," said Willa, "because I have this compass." She held the round, shiny compass in her palm so that all the WellieWishers could see it.

"How does it work?" asked Kendall.

"See the arrow?" said Willa. "It points north, and that's our way home. Aunt Miranda once told me that the playhouse is in the north corner of the garden. It won't take long to get there."

"I hope not," muttered Emerson. Her shoulders and her mouth and even the flowers on her hat looked droopy.

"Come on," said Willa. "Follow me." Willa used her trusty compass and led the WellieWishers through the trees, in the direction the arrow was pointing. Soon, they saw the playhouse. Carrot the Bunny was waiting for them.

"Hooray!" cheered Ashlyn and Camille.

"Carrot looks *hoppy* to see us!" joked Kendall.

"At last," sighed Emerson.

Willa took granola bars out of her backpack. Ashlyn filled cups with cool, refreshing water from Willa's canteen.

"Thanks for the snacks, Willa," said the girls. But before anyone bit a bite of her granola bar—

"Look!" shouted Willa, jumping up. "Our robin!"

All the girls leapt up.

"Where is it?" asked Camille.

"On the playhouse roof," said Willa.

"Hello, Robin!" called Ashlyn.

"Too-wheet," sang Emerson.

"Too-wheet," echoed all the girls.

Expecting the robin to answer them with a sweet tweet, they started to sing their friendly song:

Sing to us your song so sweet,
Song so sweet, song so—

"*Scrrreech!*" cried the robin. "*Scree-scraw, scree-scraw, scree-scraw!*" it shrieked at the girls. Then the robin dove at the surprised girls, squawking furiously and flapping its wings at them, as if to say, "*Go away, go away, go away!*"

"Help!" yelped the girls.

"But Robin, it's us, your *friends,*" cried Camille.

"Scree-scraw, scree-scraw, scree-scraw," scolded the robin, sounding more and more angry. Then it flew straight at the girls like an arrow shot from a bow. It flew so close that they could feel its wings stir the air. The robin dove low. The girls gasped.

It was headed *right toward Carrot's sticky-up ears!*

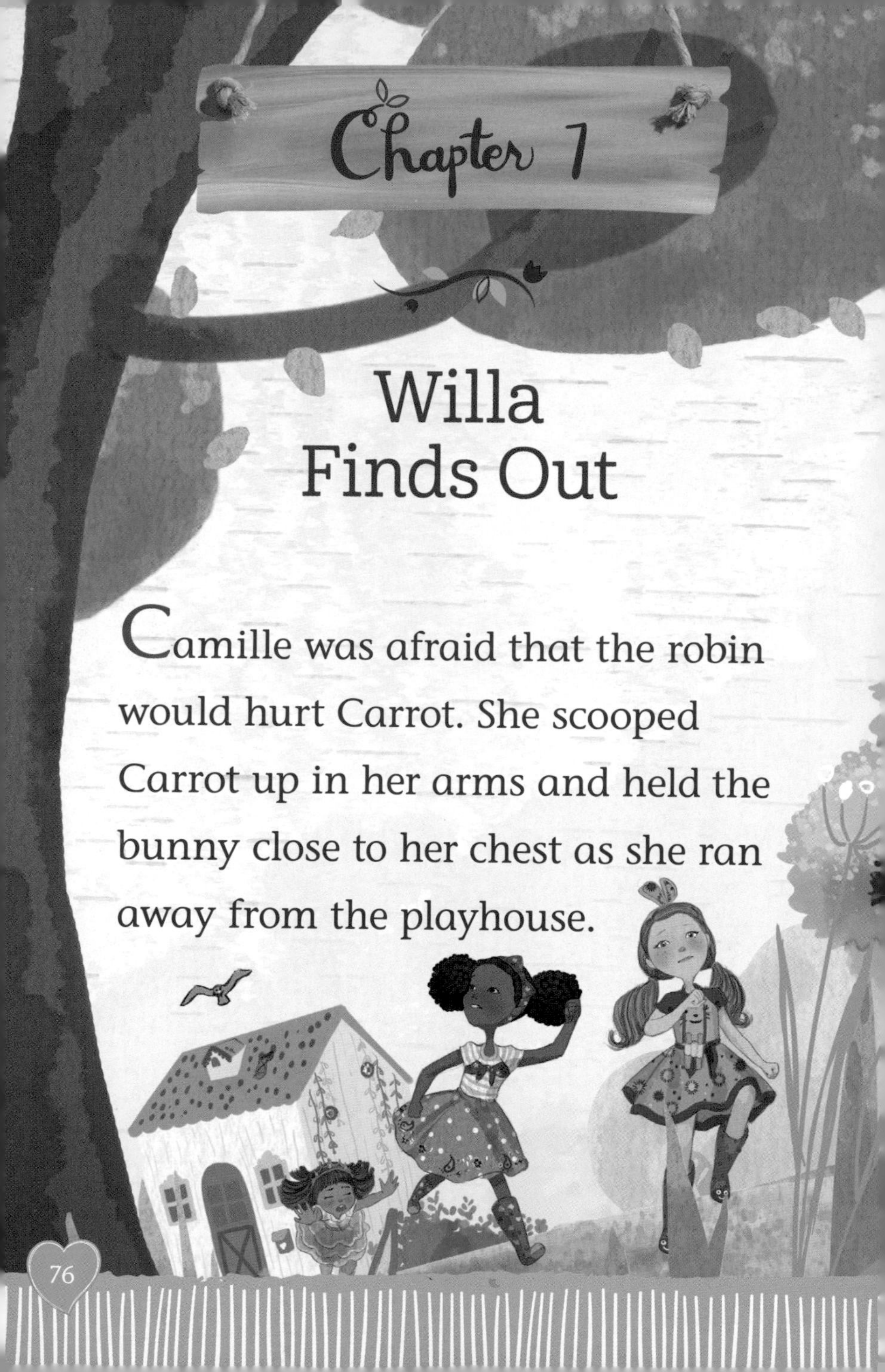

Chapter 7

Willa Finds Out

Camille was afraid that the robin would hurt Carrot. She scooped Carrot up in her arms and held the bunny close to her chest as she ran away from the playhouse.

Emerson, Ashlyn, Kendall, and Willa followed her, hurrying to get away from the robin.

Emerson's eyes filled with tears. "The robin scared me." She shuddered. "I don't like that robin anymore!"

Kendall asked Willa, "Why is the robin acting this way?"

"I don't know," said Willa in a shaky voice. Then she remembered that in her bird book, it said that when an animal's behavior changed, there was usually a good reason. What could be the reason their friend the robin had become so *un*friendly all of a sudden?

Willa gathered up all of her courage and said, "I'll go find out."

"Be careful," whispered Ashlyn.

Slowly and silently, Willa crept

back toward the playhouse. The robin cawed loudly from the roof, *"Scree-scraw!"*

Willa stood on a tree stump and peered through her binoculars. Suddenly, she gasped.

"What is it?" asked the WellieWishers.

"Oh ho!" Willa hooted. "The robin is shooing us away from the playhouse for a *very* good reason, for the best reason in the world!"

All's Well That Ends Wellie

"The robin has made a nest in Emerson's boot!" explained Willa. "And in the nest there are one, two, three, four *babies!* Our robin is protecting its family."

"Ohhhhh," the WellieWishers sighed happily.

"Baby birds in my BOOT?" squeaked Emerson.

"Your boot's a cute birdhouse, Emerson!" joked Kendall.

The WellieWishers took turns looking at the robin family through Willa's binoculars.

Ashlyn began to chuckle. "Look!" she said.

The girls all watched as the robin swooped down and pulled up a big, wiggly worm from a mud puddle. Then the robin flew up to the nest and fed the worm to the babies.

"The baby robins like their wiggly-weggly worm spaghetti," said Camille.

"That reminds me," said Emerson. "We never had *our* snack. And I'm *starving*. I'm as hungry as those baby robins!"

Suddenly, Willa understood. Just as there was a good reason why the robin's behavior had changed, there was a good reason why Emerson's had, too: She was hungry and tired! Willa smiled at Emerson and said kindly, "I'm hungry, too. Let's have our snacks."

Just then, it started to rain. The girls all crowded under a tree.

"I wish we could go inside the playhouse," said Ashlyn. "But I'm afraid we'll upset the robin."

"I have an idea," said Kendall. "The boot is over the door. If we climb in through the back window very, very quietly, we won't bother the robins."

On tiptoe, trying hard not to giggle, the girls crept around to the back of the playhouse and, one by one, climbed in the window. Once they were inside, they ate their snacks.

"Now we're all safe and happy in our nest," said Ashlyn, "just like the robin family."

Inside the cozy playhouse—very, very softly—the WellieWishers sang:

Sing to us your song so sweet:
Too-wheet, too-wheet, too-wheet!

And from the cozy nest on top of the playhouse came the sound of the robin agreeing, *"Too-wheet."*

And the four baby robins sang along happily, *"Too-wheet, too-wheet, too-wheet, too-wheet!"*

Your Backyard—for the Birds!

A yard or park offers wonderful opportunities for kids to learn about birds and show kindness and caring to their feathered friends.

In the story, Willa and the other girls learn that some birds eat seeds while other types of birds, such as robins, eat worms and bugs. Next time you and your daughter are outside in a yard, park, or nature area, look for a rock or log to turn over. What creatures are hiding beneath it? (Since you want to encourage her interest in nature—even the messy parts—if you have an urge to say "eeww," turn it into an admiring "ooooh!") If she expresses disgust or fear at the creepy-crawlies underneath, remind her that to a hungry robin, these creatures look like a delicious feast!

When she's done looking, remember to put the rock or log back in place.

Feed the Birds

These easy homemade bird treats will attract wild birds and are simple enough for young children to make with a little help.

When they're ready, hang them on branches or a deck railing. A location near bushes or trees will be more attractive to birds, who like some shelter nearby. Explain to your daughter that it may take a few days for the birds to discover the treats.

Once the birds start coming, use a bird identification book or app and find out what kinds of birds they are. Kids have great memories for names and visual details, so she'll soon be able to recognize quite a few bird species on sight.

Cereal Garland

String o-shaped breakfast cereal such as Cheerios or Froot Loops onto a length of string or yarn. Tie knots at each end, so that the cereal doesn't fall off when you hang it.

Pinecone Feeder
Tie a string to one end of a pinecone. Spread the cone with peanut butter or shortening. Roll it in birdseed. It's ready to hang.

"Dirt" Pudding
This one's for your girl, so she can eat like a bird! Make your favorite chocolate pudding recipe. Top it with crumbled chocolate graham crackers or wafers. Then set gummy worms on top. Poke a few into the pudding, so it looks like they are coming out of the ground.

Crafty Birds

Let nature inspire your daughter's creativity. The materials for this craft can be found around the house and yard or at a craft store.

You will need:

- aluminum foil
- craft glue
- tissue paper
- small leaves
- feathers
- peppercorns or black beads
- small bits of bark or cardboard
- twigs

Mold the foil into a bird shape. Glue tissue paper onto the foil to cover it. Let it dry. Glue on a layer of leaves, and let dry. Glue on feathers to make wings and a tail. For eyes, glue on peppercorns or beads, and for a beak, glue on a pointy bit of bark or cardboard. If you want the bird to stand up, poke 2 glue-tipped twigs into the body for legs, and then add a third twig toward the back. Display the bird on a shelf or windowsill.

About the Author

VALERIE TRIPP says that she became a writer because of the kind of person she is. She says she's curious, and writing requires you to be interested in everything. Talking is her favorite sport, and writing is a way of talking on paper. She's a daydreamer, which helps her come up with her ideas. And she loves words. She even loves the struggle to come up with just the right words as she writes and rewrites. Ms. Tripp lives in Maryland with her husband.